For Tristan,
with love,

na

Aug. 1992.

The Magic Flute

text by Linda Rogers, based on the opera by Mozart

illustrated by Catherine Marcogliese

The Porcupine's Quill

for my singing boys, Rick and Sasha, and for Anthony

This story takes place in an enchanted land, where sweet smelling flowers bloom all year round and every tree is laden with fruit – where precious gems tumble out of cracks in the mountains and flashing rivers toss up rings and brooches forged underwater by fairy goldsmiths.

In the kingdom of constant sunlight and summer, there is plenty to eat and drink. The fairies in charge of entertainment welcome every traveller.

There is only one discordant note in this happy place. The Queen of the Night, sovereign of the neighbouring realm, wants to take over all the lands surrounding her own. She wants to be queen of the day and the night and she will stop at nothing to get what she wants.

Unaware of the shadow cast by the evil Queen, Prince Tamino, heir to yet another neighbouring realm, is hunting with his bow and arrows. His father has sent him here to test his patience. Because the animals in the magic kingdom are immortal, none of his arrows will sing true and land on target in spite of his excellent marksmanship.

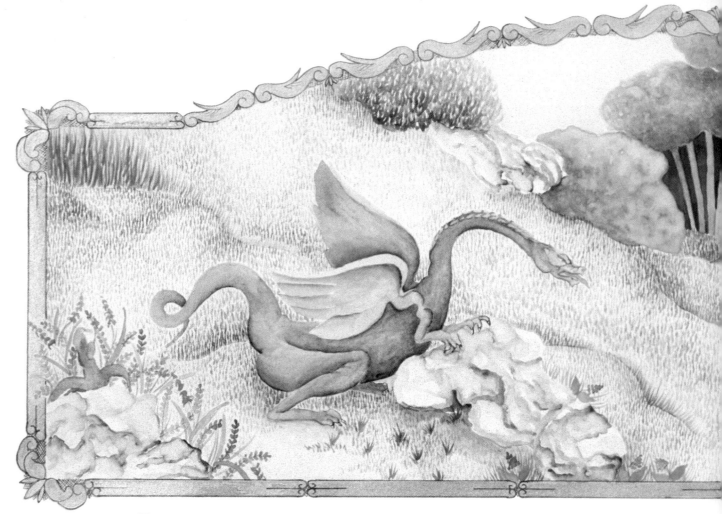

 owever Tamino is an obedient son and he persists, because he has promised to bring home venison for the royal table.

The Queen of the Night, who has reasons for wanting Tamino in her power, is watching from her side of darkness and casting a spell to trap the youth. Just as the Prince shoots his last arrow into the blinding sunlight, she sends a fire breathing serpent from her realm of sleep to chase after him.

Tamino is in mortal danger.

'Father and Mother protect me,' the normally quick and agile boy cries out in anguish, for he knows his fatigue is a handicap. 'If I had one arrow left I could

turn and shoot. Let the brute be slow and clumsy.'

The dragon is amazingly nimble. It dances up and over a rocky mountain, scorching a path through everything that grows. When the frightened youth stops to glance behind him, all he can see are flames. 'I am lost!' he laments, and the sound echoes in the mountains.

At last, exhausted, unable to carry on running over and around boulders and trees that tear at his skin and clothing, Tamino sinks into a meadow of wildflowers and gives himself up to a troubled sleep.

Screaming victory, the raging beast overtakes him.

et Tamino is protected, not by his distant and kindly parents, but by black magic. Just as the serpent is about to lick him with its tongue of fire, three masked ladies-in-waiting to the Queen of the Night arrive to save him. It is clear the Queen does not desire him to die but rather wants to make the young Prince obligated to her.

'Look!' they rejoice in unison. 'That troublesome serpent has found himself a prince to satisfy his appetite.' Understanding that the Queen intends this beautiful youth to take her daughter, Pamina, away from the wizard Sarastro, they waste no time plunging their silver spear into the dragon.

'There,' says the first lady, puffing slightly from the effort of driving her enchanted weapon through the beast's leathery armour. 'We have saved the Queen's champion. Now he will do her bidding.'

little later, with the dead serpent smoking on the ground beside him, Tamino awakens to the sound of music. There is someone near who is humming and talking to himself with a glorious accompaniment of evening songs.

'Merry I am and I am known throughout this land by old and young, lalalalala.'

It is Papageno, the birdcatcher, dressed in bright feathers and carrying a cage full of singing birds.

'Who are you?' Tamino asks the colourful fellow.

'I am Papageno and I am a very important person in this magic kingdom. I catch birds for the Queen of the Night and, in exchange, she gives me food and drink.'

'You look like a bird,' replies Tamino, shaking his head still so full of foggy sleep that he thinks he is dreaming. 'No, to be sure, I am a man,' boasts Papageno, puffing his chest like a parrot in springtime, 'and I have the strength of a giant.'

'Then you must have slain the dragon,' reasons the Prince, whose brain is slowly waking up.

'Did I? Oh yes, I did!' exclaims the birdcatcher, glad to be a hero. 'I am strong and I killed it with my bare hands.'

'Papageno!' The shrill and angry ladies show themselves to punish him for his lie.

'Today you will have fresh clear water instead of wine,' declares the first.

'And,' shrieks the second lady, if possible, more furious than the first, 'the Queen has sent you a stone instead of the usual cake.'

'Am I to eat stone?' whimpers the naughty birdcatcher, feeling sorry for himself.

'Oh yes,' rages the third lady. 'No sweet figs today. I have the honour of closing your bragging mouth with a golden lock.' She snaps it shut with pleasure and tucks the emerald key in her pocket.

'Mmmm,' mutters the sadly muzzled Papageno, 'mmmmmm.'

The ladies laugh and wag their jewelled fingers. 'That will teach your mouth full of feathers to be still next time it feels the tickle of a lie.'

aving properly punished the boastful birdcatcher, the ladies turn their attention to the handsome prince they have saved from an unpleasant experience in the stomach of a hungry dragon.

'Young man,' announces the first lady, 'my sisters and I rescued you. We are soldier maidens in the service of our sovereign, The Queen of the Night. Our silver spear rests in the side of the beast.

'The Queen has given us the privilege of delivering to a worthy gentleman this portrait of her daughter, Pamina. If you fall in love with the Princess and rescue her from Sarastro, the magician, then you will be rewarded with happiness, fortune and honour.'

Of course, Tamino feels as though he has been struck by lightning. His skin turns hot, then cold and his hair stands on end. This must be the way love happens. The Princess clearly shines like the brightest light in heaven. He presses her picture to his heart and pledges to keep her there forever.

Now it is time for the Queen of the Night to show herself in thunder and darkness and hear him promise again to save Pamina. As she appears, the earth trembles and, if the truth were known, so does Tamino, but just a little.

'Boy!' she commands in a terrible high voice and the Prince falls to his knees. 'Since I have saved you from this slaughter, you must go at once and save my daughter.' Then, in a softer voice, 'Here is a flute more precious than jewels. It will protect you and transform your sadness into merrymaking and love.'

s the Queen disappears in an explosion of stars, the ladies-in-waiting remove the birdcatcher's golden padlock. 'There, Papageno. Now remember not to lie on your journey!'

Blessed again with the gift of speech, Papageno, understanding he is to accompany Tamino on his quest for the beautiful Princess, begins to stutter excuses. 'No, I will not go. I am afraid of Sarastro. He will have me plucked and roasted and thrown to his dogs for dinner!'

'Don't be silly,' scoff all three ladies at once, handing the frightened fellow an enchanted gift. 'These silver bells will be your protection. They have all the magic you need.'

A while later, in a palace surrounded by pink roses with fierce thorns, the captive Pamina is being teased by Sarastro's fool, Monostatos. In despair, unaware that Papageno and Tamino are at this very moment struggling through the thicket to find and rescue her in the name of love, she begs to be returned to her mother, the Queen of the Night.

Monostatos answers with mocking laughter.

'Never, never. This castle will be your home forever.'

No sooner have these ugly words tumbled from his mouth than Monostatos is properly punished. Brought to the palace by magic, Papageno, dressed like a bird and strengthened by the power of his bells, appears before them.

'Who dares bully this young woman while I am alive to avenge her?'

With a cry, Sarastro's silly servant, reduced to cowardice by the wild appearance of this peculiar creature, runs and hides and Papageno takes Pamina by the hand, and leads her into the forest.

ho are you?' demands the breathless Princess as she follows the intruder out of the palace and into the garden beyond. She is not intimidated by the appearance of a man with feathers sewn into his coat.

'I am Papageno, messenger for the starry Queen,' says the birdcatcher importantly.

'You know my mother?' Pamina claps her hands with joy.

'If you are the daughter of the Queen of the Night, yes,' he answers.

'I am indeed. I am her daughter and she is my mother.'

'Well,' Papageno deliberates, 'If you are the princess in this portrait, why do you have hands and feet? This girl, who resembles you in every other respect, has none.'

'You silly,' Pamina takes the picture from him. 'Many painters find hands and feet the hardest to draw, so they leave them out. How did you get this?'

A little hurt and embarrassed by his own rudeness, Papageno begins a careful speech. 'This morning, when I was delivering birds to your mother's palace, I came across a prince and a dead serpent.'

Papageno is dying to tell her he strangled the beast with his bare hands, but he dares not. The three ladies would more than likely materialize again to punish him for his exaggerations.

'Your mother, deciding the Prince was fair, sent your picture with the three ladies and he fell in love with it in the space of time it takes an owl to blink its eye. He has promised to rescue you from Sarastro and return you to her. I am his servant and yours also.' Papageno bows extravagantly and nearly trips on one of his long feathers.

The Princess is trying to decide if he is a fool or a scoundrel. 'Why should I trust you? What if you are an evil genius the wizard has sent to trick me.'

'No,' answers the Birdcatcher. 'I am not a genius. I am not even a husband.'

'Do you want to be a husband?' asks Pamina, who has no idea that commoners fall in love, for she is only aware that princes and princesses marry and live happily ever after.

'Oh yes, I would pluck out all my feathers for a Papagena.' This softens Pamina's heart. 'Then heaven will provide for both of us. I feel it in my bones and a princess's bones never lie.'

amino is not far behind. He too has found his way through the thicket to Sarastro's palace gate. He knocks.

The gate opens slowly, revealing an old priest dressed in dark-blue silk embroidered with suns and hemmed with pearls. 'What do you want in this Holy Place?' he asks.

'The Queen of the Night has sent me here to rescue her daughter, Princess Pamina, whom I love,' Tamino declares, his heart beating wildly in his mouth, causing his voice to quiver.

'You are a brave boy, but unworthy of entering the Temple of Wisdom ruled by my lord, the wizard Sarastro.'

'Why is that?'

'Because the Queen lies and you believe her. Pamina is not her daughter.'

'I don't care whose child she is. I must see her.'

'When you have become a man and a true prince, then you will have the right to love Pamina and not before.' The priest raises his silken sleeve and Tamino hears a sound like waves on the beach as the door closes.

ocked out of the garden and separated from his friend, Tamino sadly sits down on a giant mushroom and begins to play his magic flute. His fingers and lips are guided by fairy hands and the sound is clear and true.

Soon, all kinds of animals and birds are drawn out of their cosy hiding places as if by an invisible magnet. He is surrounded by rabbits and bears and deer and every imaginable bird – the silent and the singing kind. It seems that everyone has heard his music except his true love, lost somewhere else in the forest surrounding the castle.

Lucky Tamino. He stops to take a breath and the animals are quiet. In that fortunate silence, he hears the bells.

'Papageno!' The Prince explodes with the joyful sound of a cherry splitting in a summer rain. 'I know he is with Pamina. He must be ringing the bells to tell me they are together. I will go and find them.'

If Tamino were already wise, he would know it is best to stay where you are when lost in the forest. Instead of waiting for Papageno, he leaves, hoping to find the source of the cheerful ringing.

Pamina and Papageno, equally young and foolish, run to the sound of the flute. All the noise and commotion of the music and their feet crashing in the underbrush attracts the fool, Monostatos, and his slaves, who circle Pamina and Papageno threateningly.

They are sure to be captured.

But just in time, Papageno remembers the bells.

'Come my pretty chest of bells,
make your music, ring and ring
teach their clumsy feet to dance
and frowning mouths to sing.'

'Oh,' Pamina exclaims. 'If only music could stop every cruelty and cause everyone in the world to live in harmony.'

Enchanted by the bells, the slaves and Monostatos begin to dance
and their fearful expressions transform to mirth.

Suddenly the forest is alive with a loud fanfare of trumpets that drown out the happy bells.

The trees make space between their branches to allow golden sunlight to drive away darkness.

blast of colour, silken gowns and beautiful headdresses, waken the birds in their cosy nests to sing. A patapat of polished hooves, the drumming noise of a royal cavalry, announces the arrival of the wizard Sarastro.

'I shiver and shake,' wails Papageno, forgetting his courage and the power of the bells. 'I wish I were a mouse. I'd run and hide.'

'Never mind, Papageno,' the Princess declares. 'I will tell him exactly what happened and the truth will protect us.'

As Sarastro approaches with his retinue of priests in fine cloth blessed with light by the sun, Pamina lowers herself to a respectful position and begins to speak.

'This is my doing, my lord. I ran away to join my mother who loves me dearly. Surely it is not a crime for a mother and daughter to be together.'

The wizard, touched by Pamina's loyalty, replies, 'Pamina, you are a daughter like none other and I am overjoyed. It is true that child and parent should be united and that is why you must stay with me. We are father and daughter, beautiful Princess.' He reaches a hand to her and pulls her to her feet then draws her close to him.

'Mine was a happy marriage and you were a long awaited child, born after much praying and casting of spells. It was our great joy that you were perfect, a healthy and intelligent heir to our splendid domain.

 he Queen of the Night was furious when she heard of your birth and did everything she could to spoil our happiness with diabolic tricks and witchcraft. She stole you from your mother and me when you were only a baby because she wanted to gain the kingdom of daylight, your rightful inheritance. Then she gave you a charm that made you forget any love but her own, which was guided by selfishness. My queen, your mother, died of grief.'

Meanwhile Tamino, drawn by the regal sound of the approaching wizard and his retinue and by the power of destiny, is making his way to the forest clearing, where Pamina and Sarastro are embracing one another. Father and daughter are surrounded by dazzling light.

Tamino is overwhelmed with love for the Princess. Without stopping to think of the proper behaviour on such an occasion, he reaches out to touch Pamina, who turns from her father to gaze on him and return his love.

There is no question that Pamina and Tamino were meant to be husband and wife. The whole forest is singing. All the animals and birds, even the rivers and waterfalls, make joyful noises. The only one not transported with happiness is Sarastro's servant, who leaps on the Prince.

'Oh, foolish boy.' Monostatos grabs Tamino's arm. 'How dare you touch the Princess.'

'Stop,' Sarastro cries and the fool falls back. 'Someday my daughter will marry, but not until the man who loves her proves himself. Tamino must be purified. If he can prove through trial, his ability to live in virtue and righteousness, then this land will be his.'

Sarastro holds up his arms. 'Let the trumpets sound!' And there is more music as his priests and people gather in the clearing.

'Tamino here wants my daughter in marriage. He is good and pure and nobly born. I would have him in my family, but first he must be delivered from the darkness into the light. We will destroy the spells cast upon him and his friend Papageno by the wicked queen.

'When Tamino has accepted the wisdom and power I offer, he will become my son and I will love him as my own.

'There are three trials,' Sarastro explains carefully, so there will be no misunderstanding. 'The first and possibly most difficult is this: You may look at your beloved, but you may not speak. If you do, you will lose your chance for happiness. Under pain of death, keep silent.

'The second test is by fire and you will need all your power to endure its awful consequences.

'Finally, there will be trial by water. You must be quick to avoid drowning. It is up to you to find the courage and strength you need.'

Sarastro goes and with him, the light.

gain it is night. Tamino and Papageno, left alone to face their ordeal, fumble in the darkness. Loud thunder rumbles in the distance. Papageno's quivering knees crash into each other.

'I want my mother!'

'What did you say? I beg your pardon?' asks the Prince, whose ears were too full of the skies to hear his terrified companion.

'Nothing,' answers the man who recently bragged about killing a dragon. 'Oh, I said, I think, stand by me brother.'

'Of course I will,' Tamino replies. 'Are you frightened?'

'Well, no, yes. There are shivers running up and down my spine. It must be the cold.'

'Be a man, Papageno!' says the youth bravely.

'I wish I were a girl.' Papageno is remembering the bravery of Princess Pamina.

Two priests appear in a flash of golden light. 'Are you ready to fight, my boy?' asks the first.

'Who me?' Papageno looks around as if there were another there in his place. 'Well, no. Fighting isn't my line. I'm a simple man.

I like to sleep and eat. Of course I'd also like to catch a wife.'

'You'll never get one if you refuse to undergo our trials.'

'I'll stay single then,' the birdcatcher swiftly decides.

'Too bad. Sarastro has one chosen. A pretty girl all dressed in feathers, like you,' teases the second priest in a tone of high seriousness.

'Just like me? Is she young?'

'Very.'

'Is her name Papagena?'

'Mmmm.'

'Let me just see her. Then I'll decide.'

'You may see her,' the first declares, 'but remember, you may not speak to her. Likewise Tamino may see his Princess, but he must not utter a word. If he does, he will lose her.'

The priests then disappear again.

Tamino and Papageno wander the forest waiting for the test. It isn't long before they are tempted to speak. The ladies-in-waiting to the Queen of the Night show themselves within the short space of time it takes Papageno to realize he is hungry. He begins to fidget and mumble.

'Shhh,' Tamino pinches his arm.

am not talking to them. I am talking to myself,' the birdcatcher pouts. 'Shhh!'

'Lalala,' Papageno, defiant, begins to sing. 'Shhh.'

'What are you doing in this frightful place?' the first lady asks and Papageno, naturally, begins to answer. 'We....'

'Be quiet,' Tamino interrupts before he has a chance to finish a word. 'You will spoil our chances by breaking our vows and speaking to these ladies, who are only tempting you.'

It goes without saying the ladies know of the trials and are quite malicious in their intention to start a conversation.

'Our Queen is near and she knows what you've been up to. Be warned that anyone who has business with Sarastro will burn in hell forever,' the second lady speaks bitterly, because she knows they have lost the trust of the two young men.

'Oh, Tamino, is it true?' Papageno grabs his sleeve.

'Hush. Give up this chattering or we are lost. Be strong in spirit, Papageno, and you will be rewarded.'

The ladies scowl and blink as a blinding light announces the presence of the priests of Sarastro.

'Well done, Tamino. You are steadfast and true. As for your friend....'

'Oh, I faint,' wails Papageno. 'It's too hard. I'm losing my desire for a wife.'

The priests are kindly. It is their wish that Papageno and Tamino will be strengthened and pass the tests. 'Sarastro has asked that we return to you the magic flute and your chest of bells. He also sends this table of food to ease your thirst and hunger. Refresh yourselves.' They wave their jewelled wands and a table laden with good things to eat appears before them.

'Tamino, have courage. Your goal is near. Papageno!' they put their fingers to their lips. 'Be quiet!' They vanish.

Tamino is not hungry. He puts the flute to his lips and dreams of the beautiful Princess. Papageno thinks only of his stomach.

'Go ahead. Play your flute. I'm going to put my mouth on these good things. Mmmm.'

Tamino's beautiful music serves him well. Pamina hears it and follows the sound. 'Thank you for guiding me back magic flute. Tamino, my love, I am here!'

amino does not answer. He turns away to banish the impact of her beauty and the power of her love.

'Tamino, speak to me.'

He cannot. His heart is twisted in a terrible knot.

'Oh, worse than insult, worse than death. Love's happiness is past. The light is gone from my heart. Tamino see these tears. If you do not love me, I will die.'

Poor Tamino must not answer his heartbroken Princess. It tears him to pieces but he knows he will lose her if he gives in.

After several minutes of painful struggle between the two lovers, one distraught, the other tormented, there is another trumpet flourish and Sarastro speaks.

'Tamino, your behaviour so far has been manly and composed. Now you have two further dangerous paths to take. May luck be with you. Pamina, bid him farewell.'

'Shall I never see you again?' asks the uncomprehending Princess.

'You will meet again in bliss,' Sarastro reassures his suffering daughter.

'But what of the danger?' Pamina begins to understand, but she is frightened.

'The magic flute and your love will protect me.' Tamino speaks at last.

'If you loved me as I love you, you would not go so calmly,' she insists.

'I do, but I know my duty, Pamina. We will meet again.'

Papageno is still busying himself eating and drinking at the table. He has hardly noticed that Tamino is gone. 'Glorious! Divine! Now I am in such good spirits I would fly to the sun if I had wings. There is only this funny little knock in my heart. If I had a wife, everything would be perfect. I would be happy as a prince.'

Naturally, because this is an enchanted place, the beautiful Papagena, disguised as an old crone, hears him. She appears, leaning on her stick. 'Here I am, my angel.'

'The old girl has taken pity on me, but this is too much.'

'My angel, if you promise to love me tenderly, you will see how good a wife I can be.'

'Wife? Oh my. I hate to hurt her feelings.' He speaks to her directly. 'Not so fast, my dear one. This requires careful consideration.'

'Papageno,' the old lady warns him. 'Do not hesitate or you will be lost. You will live on bread and water and never have a friend, let alone a wife to cherish.'

'Bread and water?' He hesitates. As usual Papageno's stomach rules his heart. 'Ugh! All right. I'll take your hand, but I wish it were smooth and free of wrinkles. I pledge to be true to you.' The birdcatcher bites his tongue.

'You swear?'

'Yes.' On that word the hideous old crone transforms into a lovely girl dressed just like Papageno in bright feathers.

'Pa, Pa, Pa, Papagena!' he cries, recognizing his future wife.

I t is a new day. The sun is rising, held up in the sky by joyous fairies who are singing, 'It is morning. The sun rises on its golden course. A noble peace is filling the hearts of men and women everywhere. The earth will soon become a peaceful kingdom.'

This happiness is not shared by Pamina, who is worried about her missing Prince, sure he will never return safely to her.

The fairies hear her weeping and fly to her. 'Dear maiden, look at us and remember Sarastro's promise. Tamino will triumph over evil and you will be his bride. It won't be long.'

'Follow us and you will see how your love protects him from danger.'

Pamina is taken to a place between two mountains, one spitting water and the other spouting fire. Two men in black armour are warning Tamino.

'He who wanders here will be made pure by fire and water. If you can pass through and overcome your fear, you will soar to eternal happiness.'

'I am not afraid,' answers the brave young man. 'I gladly follow.'

Pamina cannot control herself. 'Stop, Tamino. I must see you!'

'Do I hear Pamina?' the Prince asks the guards.

'You do.'

'May I speak with her?'

'You may.'

'If she is not afraid, we will endure the final trials together!'

amino and Pamina meet at the place where fire and water intersect and decide to endure the test side by side. 'Play your magic flute,' the princess requests, 'and we will pass through danger unharmed as the thousand year old tree endures lightning and thunder and rain. Music will protect us from harm.'

No sooner does she finish speaking than a branch of lightning streaks across the sky igniting the trees and grasses in the valley between the mountains. Tamino and Pamina have no choice but to go ahead. Together, they enter a wall of flame. They are blinded by smoke and overwhelmed by the intense heat. Pamina holds Tamino's cloak with one hand and wipes the tears from her eyes with the other.

Just as a burning log falls in front of them, Tamino lifts the magic flute to his parched lips and plays. It is a lovely song that sounds effortless, as if it plays itself. After a few phrases, the sky opens up and a cloudburst drenches the ravenous fire. Steam as dense as smoke boils off the rocks and the lovers almost lose each other in their slippery scramble to safety on the other side.

But the trial is not finished. The refreshing rain becomes a deluge. Rivers boil over and waterfalls plunge into madness, a flood that almost overtakes them. Pamina and Tamino, holding each other and the flute, search for a safe place. After much difficulty, they take refuge in a cave and he plays again.

This time there is a real calm. The fire is finished, the storm over. All is peaceful. The exhausted but happy pair know they have passed the tests with the help of the magic flute. Pamina and Tamino walk out into the light and watch a rainbow stretch from the place where they stand to the feet of Sarastro who has been waiting on the other side.

arastro is magnificent in his ceremonial robes embroidered with sunlight. A happy swell of trumpets and bells announces this wonderful occasion and the wizard begins to speak, 'A blessing on you my children. Your happiness is my joy.'

It is their wedding day. Two happy couples are to be joined in marriage, a ceremony the wizard himself performs at his palace, transformed by flowers for this most important day. The smell of gardenias and roses almost overwhelms delicious odours from the royal kitchen, where dozens of minor wizards are concocting beautiful delicacies to delight the brides and bridegrooms and their guests.

Exotic birds have donated special feathers for the wedding outfits of Papageno and Papagena. Pamina is dressed in silk with satin ribbons and her bridegroom is wearing royal velvet. Everyone is lost in happiness. All but one.

The Queen of the Night is not invited.

Glowering behind the garden wall, overhearing the joyful noise, she is consumed with anger. She has lost her daughter and her inheritance and been defeated by the forces of light. Beaten, but unwilling to admit it, she utters magic incantations and uses all her strength to conjure up some darkness.

It is a pitiful small sadness she makes to spoil this perfect morning. All she can muster is a little black cloud that crosses the sky and covers the sun for a single moment.

Furious, she stamps her foot and disappears into a crack in the earth, taking her three ladies with her.

Sarastro is the only one to notice. The others are so busy celebrating, they do not see the small spot on the sun or hear the awful squeal of the disappearing Queen.

However, they do stop and cheer when the wizard speaks.

'Rejoice! The sun has driven away the night. Beauty and wisdom will prevail in our garden of delight and we will all live happily ever after in perfect harmony.'

Copyright © Linda Rogers
and Catherine Marcogliese, 1992.

Published by The Porcupine's Quill, Inc.,
68 Main Street, Erin, Ontario NOB 1TO
with financial assistance from The Canada
Council and the Ontario Arts Council.

Distributed by The University of Toronto
Press, 5201 Dufferin Street, Downsview,
Ontario M3H 5T8.

Canadian Cataloguing in Publication Data

Rogers, Linda, 1944-
  The magic flute

ISBN 0-88984-129-2

1. Mozart, Wolfgang Amadeus, 1756-1791.
Zauberflöte – Juvenile literature.
2. Operas – Stories, plots, etc. – Juvenile
literature. I. Marcogliese, Catherine.
II. Title.

ML3930.M9R6
1991 j782.1'3'0269 C91-095748-7